This is for T, and for K and for M.
T is my love, the other two my best friends.

www.mascotbooks.com

Mallory Brown at Super Fun Town

For more information, please contact:
Mascot Books
560 Herndon Parkway #120
Herndon, VA 20170
info@mascotbooks.com

Library of Congress Control Number: 2017906156

CPSIA Code: PRT0717A
ISBN-13: 978-1-68401-018-9

Printed in the United States

Mallory Brown
at
Super Fun Town

Written by David Disspain

Illustrated by Tristan Tait

You may be asking yourself
about Super Fun Town
And just who is this kid named

Mallory Brown?

I'll start at the start.
That's the best spot, I'll state.
And I'll tell you right now,
so you won't have to wait.

Super Fun Town, you see,
is a really fun place.
It has big giant lizards
and green men from space.

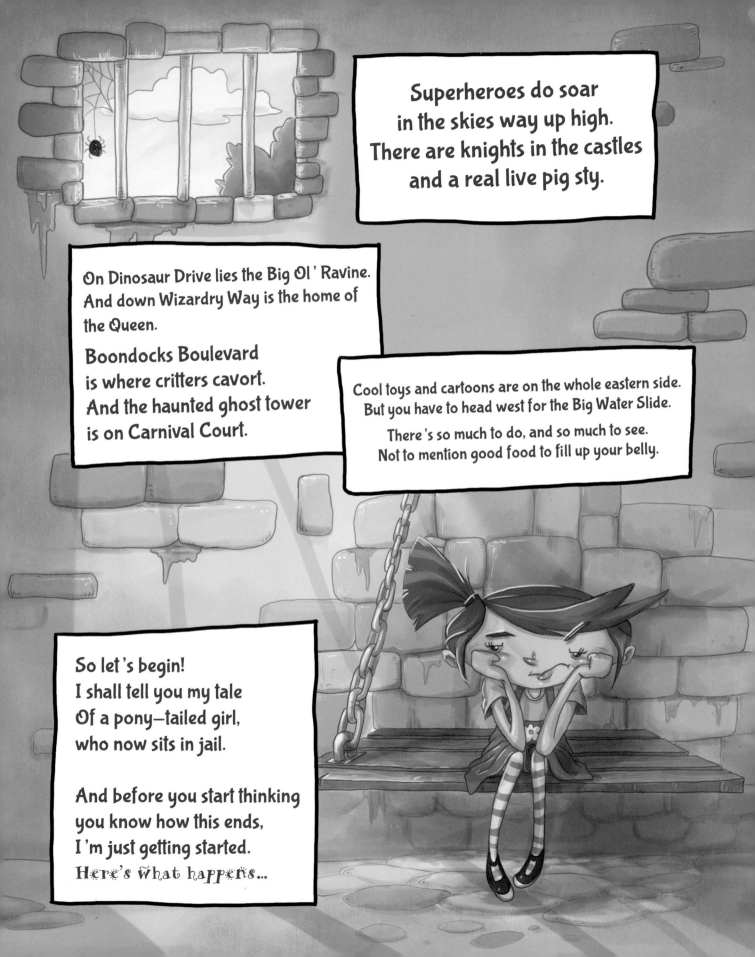

Superheroes do soar
in the skies way up high.
There are knights in the castles
and a real live pig sty.

On Dinosaur Drive lies the Big Ol' Ravine.
And down Wizardry Way is the home of
the Queen.

Boondocks Boulevard
is where critters cavort.
And the haunted ghost tower
is on Carnival Court.

Cool toys and cartoons are on the whole eastern side.
But you have to head west for the Big Water Slide.

There's so much to do, and so much to see.
Not to mention good food to fill up your belly.

So let's begin!
I shall tell you my tale
Of a pony-tailed girl,
who now sits in jail.

And before you start thinking
you know how this ends,
I'm just getting started.
Here's what happens...

Mallory Brown is her name.
She's the one in this story.
She's smart as a whip and
likes things that are gory.

Hanging from monkey bars,
feet up and head down,
She asked Dad and Mom to
go to Super Fun Town.

Her parents agreed. To her
ears, that was pleasin'.
She'd been well behaved
and that was the reason.

That night after goulash,
too excited to rest,
She stared out the window—
the one that faced west.

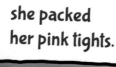
she packed
her pink tights.

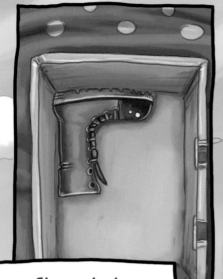

She packed
her big boots,

She packed fuzzy socks
for the cool coastal nights.

Everything neat and tidy
inside her suitcase.
Each place had a thing,
and each thing had a place.

With everyone ready,
they finally left home.
Dad had just washed the car
and polished the chrome.

Every minute seemed endless,
every mile seemed longer.
As they crossed many states,
their desire grew stronger.

They stayed at hotels and they
stayed inside inns

Until they drove up to the park,
where our story begins...

The Browns were up front,
near the start of the line,
As they waited to enter,
they were feeling quite fine.

Little Mallory Brown smiled
her biggest, best smile.
It was worth every minute,
every unbearable mile.

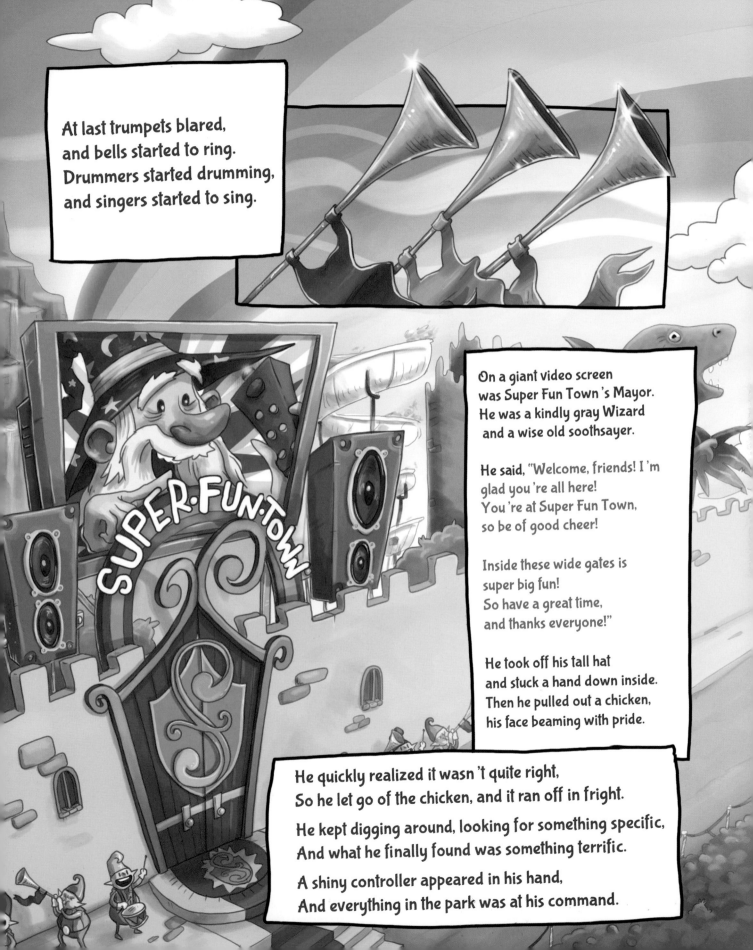

At last trumpets blared,
and bells started to ring.
Drummers started drumming,
and singers started to sing.

On a giant video screen
was Super Fun Town's Mayor.
He was a kindly gray Wizard
and a wise old soothsayer.

He said, "Welcome, friends! I'm
glad you're all here!
You're at Super Fun Town,
so be of good cheer!

Inside these wide gates is
super big fun!
So have a great time,
and thanks everyone!"

He took off his tall hat
and stuck a hand down inside.
Then he pulled out a chicken,
his face beaming with pride.

He quickly realized it wasn't quite right,
So he let go of the chicken, and it ran off in fright.

He kept digging around, looking for something specific,
And what he finally found was something terrific.

A shiny controller appeared in his hand,
And everything in the park was at his command.

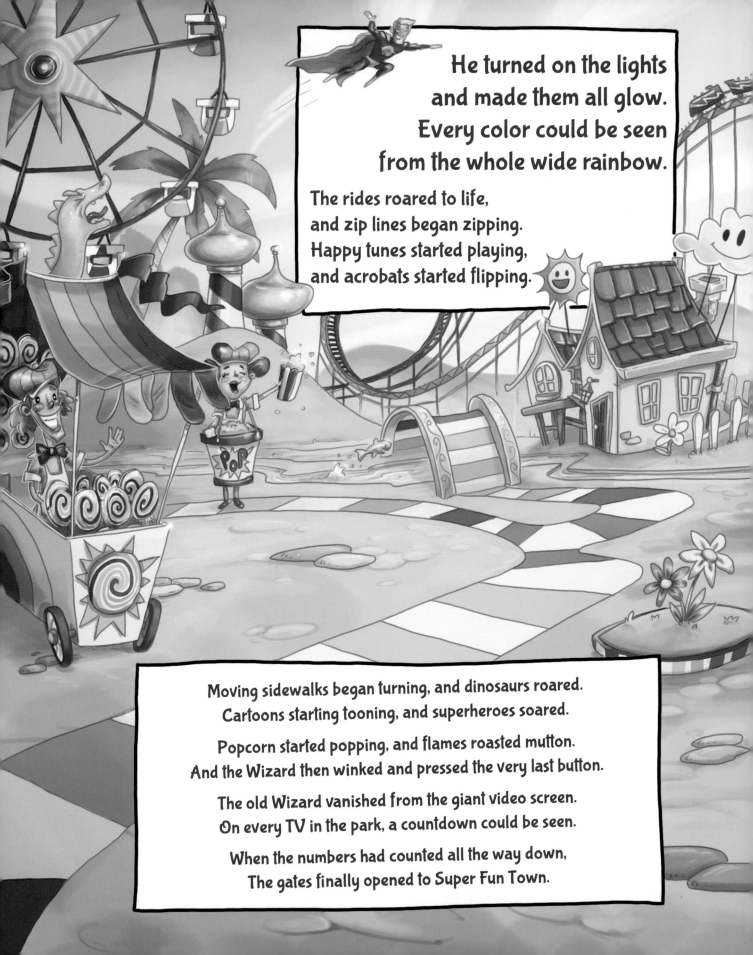

He turned on the lights
and made them all glow.
Every color could be seen
from the whole wide rainbow.

The rides roared to life,
and zip lines began zipping.
Happy tunes started playing,
and acrobats started flipping.

Moving sidewalks began turning, and dinosaurs roared.
Cartoons starting tooning, and superheroes soared.

Popcorn started popping, and flames roasted mutton.
And the Wizard then winked and pressed the very last button.

The old Wizard vanished from the giant video screen.
On every TV in the park, a countdown could be seen.

When the numbers had counted all the way down,
The gates finally opened to Super Fun Town.

At last Mal was in, and she ran through the streets,
Dodging and weaving like the world's best athletes.

Like a seasoned explorer, she moved through the crowds.
The day was sunshiny without any clouds.

The Browns went everywhere and explored every corner.
They saw each nook and cranny, and the town's every border.

They rode all the rides and ate all the foods.
They travelled by trolley, spaceship, and canoe.

At the end of the day was a fireworks show.
But unfortunately after, it was then time to go.

They had had so much fun they never wanted to leave!
And that's when Mal used the first trick up her sleeve.

The Browns wanted to stay. They weren't quite through.
They had quite a discussion about just what to do.

It didn't seem like a big deal. The park didn't need extra money.
So the Browns would sleep over
and have a tale that was funny.

Mal thought of the Castle
as the first place to stay.
But the Security Knights
would soon discover that play.

Big Dinosaur Island
was next on her list.

But the tree houses were better
and more easily missed.

So way up in the branches,
up above Super Fun Town,
they watched and they waited
for the park to shut down.

Very slowly but surely people
vanished from sight,
Leaving only the Browns in
Super Fun Town that night.

With the park gates now closed, quiet fell everywhere.
Dad brushed his teeth while Mom brushed her hair.

But Mallory dreamed that soon she'd live here.
So she considered her plans for the upcoming year.

She wanted to stay here for the rest of her life.
She'd live in the big Castle and be Charming's first wife.

She'd ride dolphins and ponies until old with wrinkles,
And eat blue cotton candy and doughnuts with sprinkles.

Now with Mom softly snoring and Dad curled in a ball,
Mal unrolled her maps so she could see one and all.

She examined the streets, down to every last inch.
She wanted more options if she got caught in a pinch.

With her schemes all arranged and everything right,
She lay down in the treetop to sleep for the night.

Overnight she dreamed of pink glitter and glory.

When she awoke the next day
is where we continue our story.

She told her plan to her parents
as dawn finally broke.
They thought she was kidding
 or telling a joke.

But as they listened
to her spell out her ploy
On how to stay in the park,
they felt nothing but joy.

Her gambit was feisty,
although a bit innocent.
They didn't want to admit it,
but her plan was brilliant.

Against better judgment,
they said they'd give it a try.
Dad had a great lawyer,
the best money could buy.

Since the next day had dawned
and the park was prepared,
They left the big tree house
to avoid being ensnared.

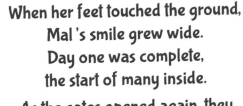

When her feet touched the ground,
Mal's smile grew wide.
Day one was complete,
the start of many inside.

As the gates opened again, they
blended in with the others.
Just like similar families
with grandmas and brothers.

The Browns kept on going
like nothing was wrong.
They started riding the rides
and playing ping pong.

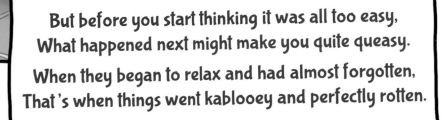

But before you start thinking it was all too easy,
What happened next might make you quite queasy.

When they began to relax and had almost forgotten,
That's when things went kablooey and perfectly rotten.

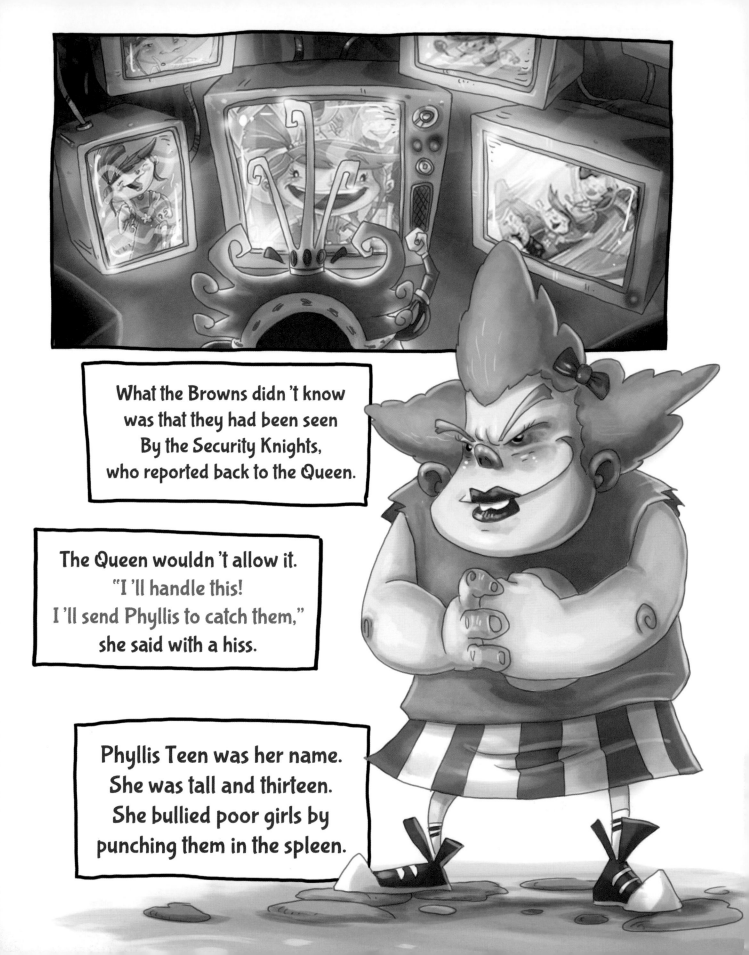

What the Browns didn't know
was that they had been seen
By the Security Knights,
who reported back to the Queen.

The Queen wouldn't allow it.
"I'll handle this!
I'll send Phyllis to catch them,"
she said with a hiss.

Phyllis Teen was her name.
She was tall and thirteen.
She bullied poor girls by
punching them in the spleen.

"Hey, little girl," she commanded,
"come over here now!"
But Mal shook her head.
There was no way, no how.

When Miss Teen's tiny brain
finally processed the denial,
She chased little Mal
to put her on trial.

Mal ducked and dodged without letting up.
Phyllis Teen was so angry, she got a case of hiccups.

But Phyllis wouldn't give up, not from this little hitch.
Her anger grew bigger, and her eyes started to twitch.

She kept up the pursuit and never stopped tracking,
Even with her hiccups that sounded like quacking.

Mallory knew what to do. There was only one way to stop her:
By using a mallet from the Prairie Dog Popper.

She bopped Phyllis Teen right on top of her head,
And the Knights had to carry her right off to bed.

The Queen watched from above as Phyllis Teen fell.
She fumed with defeat and wanted to yell.

As she watched people passing, way down below,
An idea came to mind, full of guts and gusto.

The Queen needed a trap that Mal wouldn't see
And a good way to catch her,
so she'd be unable to flee.

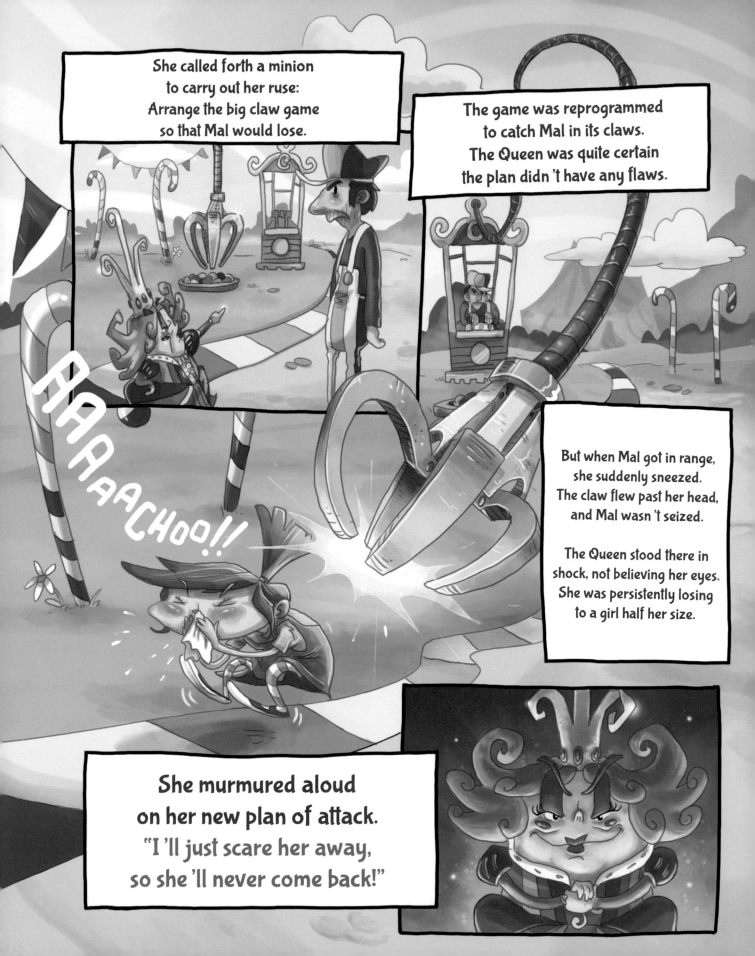

The Queen made a deal
with the ghosts where they haunted,
For she knew scaring people
was what the ghosts wanted.

The ghosts couldn't shake
on their sinister pact.
So they signed in ghost ink
on their phantom contract.

As Mal walked around
with her parents in tow,
She had no idea
of what would be the next show.

The Browns ambled along
in front of Ghost Tower,
And the Queen's menacing plan
displayed its true power.

The apparitions poured out
from the Tower's windows and doors.
They came down from the ceilings
and up through the floors.

Onto Carnival Court
they spilled out like a horde,
Shrieking and screaming
and scaring as they roared.

Mal scowled at the ghosts.
She simply wasn't impressed.
The Browns had come way too far to be so easily stressed.

It was clear that the ghosts
were fake and plugged in,
So she unplugged the power
and they were gone with the wind.

The Knights had to report
about their big loss.
They didn't want to see her—
their big evil boss.

But the Security Queen
was one step ahead,
And was already working
on a new plan instead.

She sent out the Toy Soldiers to capture her prey.
"Bring her to me! I want her here by midday!"

They wound themselves up to follow her orders
And went into the streets, crossing all the town's borders.

Mallory saw them coming with
their brightly colored clothes...

And washed them away
with a big **fire hose.**

But the spray was too strong.
She lost control of the stream!
Her parents floated away
into the hands of the Queen.

"Take them away!" the Queen ordered. "At once!"
And for the very first time, Mal felt like a dunce.

As they were carried away,
she got one last peek.
This was all unexpected,
and it left her quite weak.

In the grip of the Queen
her parents were trapped.
Now a new plan was needed.
She'd have to adapt.

Mal needed a way
to free her daddy and mommy.
"I know what I'll do!" she said.
"I'll go ask the Swami!"

For the Swami was wise
and could forecast the future,
He had the true power
and was not just a moocher.

She found the wise Swami at the top of his rope,
And what he might tell her gave her new hope.

With his hands to his temples, he entered a trance,
Using his Swami talents to give the future a glance.

"I see it all very clearly,
like it was on the TV!
She's kidnapped the Wizard,
and other bad things I see!

She's threatened all the Knights
to obey her commands,
And she's tricked all the ghosts
to meet her demands.

She's seen all of the clowns
without their clown noses.
She's changed all the locks
and animal shrubbery poses.

She's hoarding red apples
and red applesauce.
She's stolen old magic
that makes her the boss.

With all that she's done,
and all she can still do,
She needs someone to stop her.
That someone is you!"

The Swami opened
his eyes and said,

"That's all I can tell.

I wish I could help you,
but she's trapped me as well."

The news of the Queen left Mal shocked and quite sad.
She had no idea that the Queen was so bad.

Mallory needed time to gather up her thoughts.
Her stomach felt twisted and tied up in knots.

The Swami also saw that
Mal was terribly upset
And needed some help
so she wouldn't just fret.

"I may not be able to
come down from this rope,
But that doesn't mean
you're left without hope.

All you need is a way to
beat her at her own game,
To trap her or trick her and
show she is to blame.

You must expose all her secrets.
Leave her nothing to hide!
Get the whole town behind you.
They'll be on your side!"

Mallory was determined to follow this suggestion.
But how to outsmart the Queen? Now that was the question!

Freeing the Wizard was her only true course,
So she asked one more question of her only resource.

"Where's the
Wizard now?"
Mallory asked her mentor.

"He's inside the Castle,"
said the Swami,

"right in the center!"

"Don't worry Sir Swami, I'll rescue him quick!
She won't get away with this mean little trick!"

The Swami then waved and wished her good luck,
Hoping he and the Wizard would soon be unstuck.

As Mal made a new plan,
she stopped for a snack.
The Queen saw where Mal was
and launched an attack.

She freed all the beasts in the huge petting zoo,
And down Snorkel Street they galloped and flew.

As the animals came charging, Mal ran from the stampede.
Then she made a sharp left at her very top speed.

The Water Slide ended in a big blue lagoon,
And that's where all the animals ended up soon.

But instead of being mad after their long pointless dash,
They all swam and played at a pool party bash.

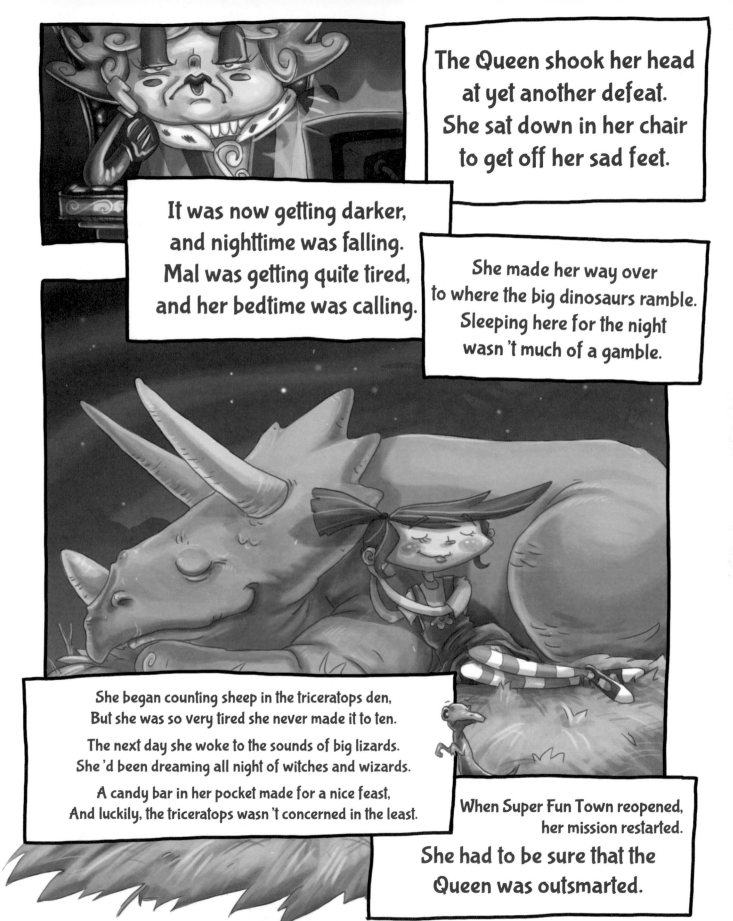

The Queen shook her head
at yet another defeat.
She sat down in her chair
to get off her sad feet.

It was now getting darker,
and nighttime was falling.
Mal was getting quite tired,
and her bedtime was calling.

She made her way over
to where the big dinosaurs ramble.
Sleeping here for the night
wasn't much of a gamble.

She began counting sheep in the triceratops den,
But she was so very tired she never made it to ten.

The next day she woke to the sounds of big lizards.
She'd been dreaming all night of witches and wizards.

A candy bar in her pocket made for a nice feast,
And luckily, the triceratops wasn't concerned in the least.

When Super Fun Town reopened,
her mission restarted.
She had to be sure that the
Queen was outsmarted.

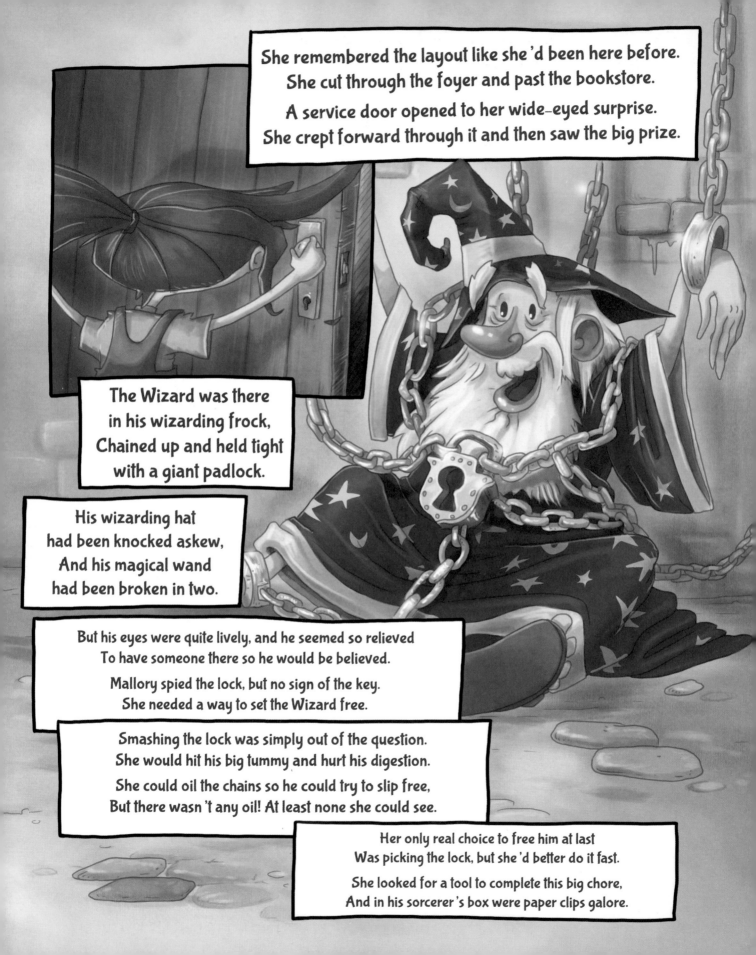

She remembered the layout like she'd been here before.
She cut through the foyer and past the bookstore.

A service door opened to her wide-eyed surprise.
She crept forward through it and then saw the big prize.

The Wizard was there
in his wizarding frock,
Chained up and held tight
with a giant padlock.

His wizarding hat
had been knocked askew,
And his magical wand
had been broken in two.

But his eyes were quite lively, and he seemed so relieved
To have someone there so he would be believed.

Mallory spied the lock, but no sign of the key.
She needed a way to set the Wizard free.

Smashing the lock was simply out of the question.
She would hit his big tummy and hurt his digestion.

She could oil the chains so he could try to slip free,
But there wasn't any oil! At least none she could see.

Her only real choice to free him at last
Was picking the lock, but she'd better do it fast.

She looked for a tool to complete this big chore,
And in his sorcerer's box were paper clips galore.

To call it a dungeon
was a bit glorified.
It was more like a hallway
with rooms on one side.

In cell number one
sat a glum little clown
All alone by himself,
his face a sad frown.

And in cell number two sat her mom and her dad.
She'd never seen her parents look quite that sad.

Mal ran to the bars to make sure they were well,
but she had to keep moving until inside her own cell.

In cell number three the Wizard was placed.
They locked him up quickly, with no time to waste.

Mallory then came last.
She kept her eyes on the floor.
The alien soldiers put her
in cell number four.

The cell door clanged shut
with an awful loud slam,
And little Mallory knew
she was in quite a jam.

But she would never give up, and she would never give in.
She just needed a way to turn this loss into a win.

As she sat in the cell, she looked everywhere
For a way to escape and get away from this scare.

But before she discovered
a good way to get free,
The Queen stood at the door,
twirling the key.

"Well, well, well," the Queen giggled,
"what do we have here?
A tiny young thing
filled with all kinds of fear?

You've been terribly naughty
and caused quite a riot.
But that's all over now,
and it's time for some quiet."

It was right at that time
Mal remembered the hat.
It lay there before her,
just like a door mat.

She picked it up quickly
before the Queen spoke anew
And reached deep inside it,
hoping for some kind of clue.

But what her hand came across was something quite unexpected.
She knew the Wizard had a plan, just like she'd suspected.

All Mal needed now
was to make the Queen even bolder
And get her to brag
about what the Swami had told her.

The Queen needed to talk
and tell all of her stories.
And Mal wanted to hear
the Queen boast of her glories.

So she began asking questions
to get the Queen started.
If the Queen didn't talk,
then she couldn't be outsmarted.

"So you kidnap families and little girls and clowns,
What else have you done to rule Super Fun Town?"

The Queen laughed out loud—it was a big hearty snicker.
"I'll just show you," she said. "It will be so much quicker!"

From out of her pocket
came a clear crystal ball.
She held it close to the bars
so Mal could see it all.

It showed the Queen breaking
nearly every single rule.
It showed her being mean
and wicked and cruel.

Everything the Swami had told her
was true and was right.
All the stealing and hoarding,
right there in plain sight.

When the Queen then looked up, she expected a frown
On the face of her foe, little Mallory Brown.

But instead of a grimace on little Mallory's face,
There was a huge smile spread right there in its place.

From the old Wizard's hat, in Mal's fist she had squeezed—
His remote controller to change all the TVs.

Mal had switched every TV to the same exact station,
And what the Queen said had shown at every location.

Everyone in Super Fun Town
heard what the Queen said,
And everyone knew
they had all been misled.

The people were angry
at all the Queen's choices.
They shouted and yelled
in their most angry voices.

They wanted the Queen
to be captured and held.
They wanted her out
and quickly expelled.

Inside the Castle, the Queen still didn't know That Mallory's actions had put on quite a show.

"Why are you smiling? You weird little brat! I caught you! I won! What do you think of that?"

Mallory just kept smiling and not saying a word. She knew everyone saw it. She knew everyone heard.

"Suit yourself," the Queen said as she started to leave.

"You've got nowhere to hide! No more tricks up your sleeve!"

There was no way to get out,
no way to go down.
She needed a way out of
Super Fun Town.

Back in the tower,
she climbed every stair.
She threw back the shutters
to the wide open air.

The very top of the tower
was filled with balloons.
Super Fun Town released them
on bright afternoons.

She would hang by their strings
and be carried away.
But she wasn't that lucky,
and this just wasn't her day.

The Wizard laughed hard
and hugged her close.
"I know that you love them.
It certainly shows!"

Their cell door was opened, and her parents were freed.
Even the clown was released, and he ran out with speed.

The Wizard held out his hand
for Mal to return his hat.
He put it back on his head
and grinned like a big cat.

"Now Mallory Brown, you've had a hard time,
But we still must address your own simple crime.

For staying in the park well after it closed,
Punishment is at hand and must be imposed.

I hereby sentence you to more time in a cell,
But this time you'll have a new cellmate as well."

As Mal heard those words,
she stared at her foe.
This was new information.
Stuff she needed to know.

It wasn't expected,
but it was true just the same.
She'd be like the Queen
if she kept playing this game.

Mal sat there and stared, and then stared some more.
She was just like the Queen, and that, Mal couldn't ignore.

And that was something she just couldn't be.
Mal needed to change, and use some inner Tai Chi.

It took all her effort to
touch the Queen's hand.
Mal said,

"Give them a call.
They might understand."

The Queen then did something she hadn't done in while. She felt herself grin. She felt herself smile.

Suddenly Mal saw that the Queen wasn't scary. And that just sitting here, she seemed quite ordinary.

As the day marched on, Mal sat in that cell
Across from the Queen and played show and tell.
Mal shared her Town maps and her plans for each day.
While the Queen's crystal ball showed Mal every hallway.

They laughed and they talked,
and they soon became friends.
They said they were sorry,
and they both made amends.

When the Wizard came in
to set Mallory free,
The Queen hugged her goodbye—
quite a sight to see!

Epilogue:

After all had grown calm, after all that big scene,
Mal came back again to visit the Queen.

They talked and they chatted and they gabbed for a day.
They kept right on talking until there was nothing to say.

The Queen's parents forgave her, and would visit her soon
In the warm summer months, probably mid-June.

The Queen couldn't use her old title in jail.
It didn't work anymore, and she couldn't get mail.

So the Queen had to whisper her real name in Mal's ear,
But what the Queen's name is, I can't tell you here.

I *can* tell you that Mal had found a true friend.
And that's very important, right here at...

The End